THE LITTLE BLACK DRESS

Tales from France

The
Little Black
Dress

Tales from France

Cary Fagan

THE MERCURY PRESS

ACKNOWLEDGEMENTS

Some of these stories have previously been published in *Blood & Aphorisms,*
Outlook, and *World Letter.*

Epigraph from "Cartes Postales" by Miklós Radnóti, in *Subway Stops,*
edited and translated by Emery George, published by Ardis.
Used by permission of the publisher.
Words in quotations on page 63 are from "Paris," by Miklós Radnóti,
translated by Steven Polgar, Stephen Berg, and S.J. Marks,
published in *Poetry East,* Number 22, Spring, 1987.

The publisher gratefully acknowledges the financial assistance of the Canada
Council and the Ontario Arts Council, as well as that of the Ontario Ministry
of Culture and Communications through the Ontario Publishing Centre.

Editor: Beverley Daurio
Cover design: Gordon Robertson
Cover illustration: Gary Clement

Composition in Bembo by TASK.
Printed and bound in Canada.

Canadian Cataloguing in Publication:

Fagan, Cary.
The little black dress
ISBN 1-55128-005-1
I. Title.
PSPS8561.A42L58 1993   C813'.54   C93-093399-0
PR9199.3.F336L58 1993

Canadian Sales Representation: The Literary Press Group.

The Mercury Press is distributed in Canada by General Publishing,
and in the United States by Inland Book Company (selected titles).

The Mercury Press
137 Birmingham Street
Stratford, Ontario
Canada
N5A 2T1

AUTHOR'S NOTE

Most of these stories were written
on a short trip to France in January, 1991.

for Joanne,
my real country

Throw that awful paper away: Notre-Dame
is waving a cheerful cloud, white as a lamb.
Think of nothing else: sit down, look around,
observe! for tomorrow, above the square,
grey dawn will surely break without you there.

— Miklós Radnóti

CONTENTS

The sky is dark; there are lights on in the apartments across the Rue Serpente; we close the enormous curtains. At what point does the old life slip away and the new life begin? One waits for it, despairs of it, watches it not pass and not pass again...

The Little Black Dress

MY HUSBAND SAID: "How can someone as intelligent as you care so much about fashion?"

We stood in the light of a show window on the Rue de Rennes. It was night and cold and we were huddled in our coats. Behind the glass was a series of faux columns and on the pedestal of each rested a single shoe. Black, violet, tan or suede, open or pointed toes, slingbacks, with high or very high heels. I kept looking at one near the front, tipped on its side.

"That shoe," I said, "is more beautiful than anything I've seen in the Louvre."

My husband shook his head. "What a crazy thing to say. All day long you've been acting strangely."

"What time does the store open tomorrow?" I asked.

He pulled his scarf around his mouth, muffling his voice. "Tomorrow we're going to see the Bibliothèque Nationale."

"Yes," I said. "But what time?"

THE FRENCH dress so much better than we do that there are really no grounds for comparison. They dress well, as it were, from cradle to grave. The babies in their gorgeous winter suits; the tiny girls in pleated skirts and patent-leather shoes; the old women, gnarled hands grasping canes, in cloth capes; and all the women in between. They were a revelation to me and I felt a very personal, very exhilarating kind of pain.

"All right, I grant you that Parisian women are good looking," my husband said, showing that he understood nothing at all. We had begun walking again, but I had stopped to evaluate a window of cashmere sweaters. He stared at me in disbelief and then said, as if taken by a fit of inspiration, "A woman like you, with all your causes and organizations. When there are people on the street dressed in rags!"

"If you're trying to evoke a sense of shame, it won't work," I said.

"What about all those authors you read?" he asked. "You know, Fay Weldon and Isabel Allende and Alice Munro. What would they say about this new obsession of yours?"

But I didn't answer. I was too busy opening my handbag to count the number of francs in my wallet.

BY PROFESSION I am an optometrist. That is, I am concerned with the health of the eye. My practice is successful enough to make scheduling holidays difficult. My husband, who builds houses, knows the names of authors only because I keep their books at my bedside; he never reads anything more subtle than carpentry manuals. He has always been proud of my "intellectual nature," which still charms me. He is a sweet man but he has an inflexible, or perhaps better, an unimaginative mind. (One need only look at the houses he builds.) The fact is I've never much noticed clothes before, back home where the opportunity for such expression is so limited. In my work I am concerned with seeing, but never with what is seen. I wear a professional white gown and crêpe-soled shoes; my patients expect it. Whenever a woman who is all dressed up comes into my office, I always think that she is trying to show off how much money her husband makes.

But here in Paris the sight of all these beautiful clothes made me dizzy, as if I'd swallowed a strong drink that surged through my body. And then, immediately afterward, came a sense of terrible loss, for no matter how much money I spent I could never, ever catch up.

This was my inventory of purchases to date:

Three pairs shoes

Two blouses (one linen, one raw silk)

One satin pouf skirt

One wool jacket (nipped-in waist)

But still I felt unsatisfied, as if I could not fully know my own desire. My husband was too basic a sort of man to sympathize with such a vague need. So naturally he could not understand when I came back to the hotel with yet another exquisitely wrapped package from the Rue St. Honoré.

"Are you planning to open a store?" he said.

Ignoring him, I untied the package. And took out what seemed even to me a very small amount of material for the figure on the price tag attached. I went to the mirror on the armoir and held against me what the magazines call the Little Black Dress. I'd never worn one before and, seeing it on a mannequin, realized that I had very few years left in which I still *could* wear it.

My husband said, "Well, it's your money," and picked up his coat.

MY HUSBAND WAS ANGRY enough to leave the hotel room and spend the afternoon by himself, although not before making plans to meet me at a restaurant for dinner. I took a long bath, carefully shaved my legs, washed and dried my hair, and then slipped the Little Black Dress over my head. The restaurant was off the Avenue Foch and when I arrived by cab he was already there waiting. He watched as the maitre d' removed my coat and I walked to his table. Leaning over the flickering candle, I could feel the Little Black Dress slide against my skin. When he spoke a deep throb came from his throat. "You look... fabulous," he said. The wine went quickly; we hardly knew what we ate. Declining coffee, we hurried back to the hotel, where he took me in his arms. We made love very slowly and, according to both our silent wishes, I never fully took off the Little Black Dress. In the late morning, when we awoke, I was still wearing it.

ONE MORNING— I mean three o'clock in the morning— we sat in an over-lit café drinking (of all things) hot milk. It was our last day breaking and we were subdued.

My husband said, "I get it now."

I wearily rubbed my eyes. "Get what?"

"The clothes thing. This buying spree. I know why you do it."

"You do?" I yawned.

"To fight death." He looked at me knowingly. "Yes," he repeated, "to fight death. Because society has made women so conscious of the aging of their bodies. You're more aware of your own mortality than men are. You see it in the mirror every day. And so you wrap yourselves up in beautiful clothes because fashion is eternally youthful. That's what you're doing, fighting death."

My husband looked at me affectionately. It was an annoying look he sometimes got. I thought of the only answer I could give.

"Today," I said, "you're going to buy me a hat."

In the square, an acrobat balanced on five chairs.
Well, we all do that, but not so elegantly.

And afterwards, the little girl in a cowboy jacket
with frills, calling: "Goodbye café, goodbye café..."

Son and Father

WHAT I REMEMBER is ice cream, a train moving fast, the wings of pigeons, and shadows on a ceiling.

It isn't very much, fragments of an otherwise unrecoverable history. But no, one can't call "history" that which is of only personal significance. And what does it even mean to me, when I could have forgotten it all for so long? Merely time past: as the saying goes, water under a bridge.

Now it is late, the hotel is quiet, and Anna is asleep in the room. Our son is sleeping too, of course, the covers probably pulled up almost over his head. The night porter dozes behind the desk, his radio turned down to a murmur. From this chair I can see the dark sidewalk beyond the glass doors, then the Rue Huysmans, then some scaffolding against the building. I wonder what our son will remember of this day. Any more than I do of that month, so many decades ago?

When I was nine years old my father took me to Europe. London, Paris, Rome. He had business to conduct for part of each day and so I played with new toys in the room or went out with a different nanny who never spoke more than a few words of English. My mother was supposed to come with us. It was only at the last moment that she and my father separated, for good. I never lived with her again.

The next time I went to Europe I was twenty-three and I believed then that it was my first time. I could not understand certain moments of unaccountable emotion that suddenly came upon me, a kind of despondent exhilaration. If I understand them now it is only because, when I first stepped onto the balcony of our hotel room and saw the city below, the past returned to me. I felt faint and had to grasp the rail.

In the last days a few memories have come back, not in a jarring way, but gently, like noticing some photographs on the wall that have always been there. I haven't told Anna. I'm not sure why, perhaps out of embarrassment for remembering so little. When my father must have done so much to make it memorable.

Or perhaps it's something else. For the strange thing, what haunts me now, is how happy I was during that month. This is not exactly a memory, being of no specific moment but just a feeling; and it has returned the way light comes in the morning. During that month I experienced a kind of bliss that an adult would never imagine possible for a child.

Of course I did not know that my mother had left us. I wasn't told until we came back, when she herself spoke to me in a restaurant. I just thought it was a temporary adventure, son and father together. I even bought postcards to bring to her— one of the "Mona Lisa" and another of the Trevi Fountain. I recall that only because I found them many years after and, not knowing where they had come from, threw them out.

What I do remember:

Ice cream for breakfast. In a café, sitting as it seemed to me, right in the middle of the street. My father said, "What would you like for breakfast, bread and jam?" He was rattling an English newspaper. I said: "No, I want ice cream." I held myself very still, as if I'd just blasphemed. My father didn't even put down the paper; he just spoke quietly to the waiter who grinned. The ice cream came in a tall glass, three flavours, with a long, cold, metal spoon. I don't remember eating; just looking at it, and the spoon in the saucer.

I remember:

A train moving fast. My hands pressed to the window as I stared breathlessly. Where were we going? What did I see flashing by the thick glass of the window? Just the rush of it, that's all.

I remember:

In a square, a great square surrounded by arches. A pretty lady, one of the hired nannies, handed me a paper sack of bread crumbs. I couldn't understand what she said but I saw by the miming of her hands. I opened the sack, put in my fingers, and tossed some crumbs on the ground at my feet. Immediately a pigeon, grey and dirty, flopped down before me. I laughed out loud. Then another, then three more, then a dozen, then a hundred, all fluttering down. I gasped and dropped the bag, spilling the rest of the crumbs, and felt the sensation of wings beating against me as I screamed and screamed. And the pretty lady picking me up in her arms, pressing me to herself and murmuring in Italian to comfort me as the pigeons whirled around us. But I wasn't afraid, I wasn't!

I remember:

Shadows on the ceiling, which I could see from my narrow bed. It was the shadow of the devil; I'd seen his picture in a museum. Horns. The devil was chattering at me— a kind of tic-tac noise from inside the wall. And I whispered: Go away, devil. Go away.

Nowhere can I see the face of my father. It is behind the newspaper, in another room. Nor do I remember missing my mother. She was far away, waiting for me, her arms open. And I felt... bliss. Afterwards, when we came home, I wasn't happy again for a long time.

Now, sitting here, I feel the night air seep in from beneath the glass doors. What will my own child remember? What does he feel? I will go up and open the door and let my shadow move across the wall. And then I will return to bed, where Anna will shift toward me without waking. In the morning I will tell her: on my first trip to Europe I was nine years old. I was alone, but I felt something nearby, keeping me safe, as if I would never die.

Then we will get up and take our son down for breakfast.

Morning and the light through the shutters the colour of pearl. Distant sound of workmen, like a heavy canvas being slapped against the ground. The stale smell of smoke on my shirt as I pull it on.

I Love Mozart

GAIL AND MONICA were not speaking to each other. They sat at their regular table at the Café Deux Garçons— at least they thought of it as theirs, whereas to the townspeople they were no more existent than the shadows of ghosts— they sat with their arms folded and legs crossed, their *cafés-au-lait* growing cold.

Gail and Monica looked like sisters, with their short straight hair, round eyes, and black skirts purchased, amidst much hysterical laughter, in a boutique on the Rue Espariat. They had been in Aix-en-Provence for six months now, having taken a year off after graduation and before joining the same accounting firm, which after all would be there for ever and ever. They had known of the Café Deux Garçons even before arriving, for Monica had read about it, and they immediately took to spending every morning there as the winter sun slanted through the high windows and illuminated the dust in the air. They loved the Deux Garçons for its splendidly high ceiling, for the pale green frieze of columns along the walls, for the sound of waiters arguing behind the swinging doors, for the gold-rimmed cups, for the genteel dowdiness.

But that was when they were speaking; before

Alfred had come between them.

"If you've forgotten your money, I'm not going to pay for you," Gail said.

Monica's reply was to pick up her cup and take a gulp.

"It's almost noon. Maybe he isn't coming."

"You are free to leave at any time," Monica said.

Neither of them stirred, but watched the waiters unrolling white linen onto the tables for the lunch trade. The first thing they had learned was how to sit as if they had no intention of ever getting up. The waiters came forward to greet a quartet of old women in fur collars and usher them to *their* table. When Gail and Monica were still talking, indeed were still best friends (which had been only two days before), they had taken endless pleasure in analyzing the clientele of the Deux Garçons. They had decided on the professions of the women's dead (yes, undoubtedly dead) husbands: a pharmacist, a notary, a church organist, and a mortician. They were certain that the hawk-nosed gentleman who wrote in a small black book took bets on the bullfights in Nîmes. And the couple who never looked at one another while their five-year-old son silently ate his *tarte tatin* had surely made a marriage of convenience, linking two aristocratic but destitute Aix families.

Gail fished about in her purse and came up with a packet of Gitanes. She pulled off the cellophane and fumbled with the matches as she tried to strike a light.

"Who are you trying to kid?" Monica said. And then a moment later, "Can I have one?"

"No. Oh, all right."

And so the two sat smoking their Gitanes at the proper angle and occasionally coughing. When Alfred arrived, an hour late, he shook hands with all the waiters and kissed the old women, once on each cheek. Then he sauntered over to their table, kissed them, and sat down.

"I am sorry to be coming late," he said in his hesitant and charming English. "What a day is today. I have to work like a beast."

He reached across the table and in one elegant motion took a cigarette, lit it, drew in a long breath, and let two lazy plumes rise from his nostrils. Every morning at six a.m. Alfred delivered the *baguettes* to the salon of the hotel where Gail and Monica lived. As he was a cousin of the manager, he often returned after his rounds for a *café* and left again, just as Gail and Monica, white-faced from sleep, were coming down the stairs. But two days ago he had lingered on and introduced himself, although whether to Gail or to Monica first was a matter of disagreement.

He finished his cigarette and took another, apparently in no hurry to speak. Yesterday morning he had been in more of a rush, bounding into the salon to tell them of the next evening's concert. "Mozart's *Requiem*," he had pronounced with reverence. "It is very great and very sad. And see, I have two tickets! The *portier* of the theatre gave them to me. He is a personal friend of mine."

He had said this with such pride that they supposed the *portier* to be just under the town mayor. What he did not say was which one of them he wanted to take. Perhaps he had simply neglected to, or couldn't make up his mind. But the way he looked at each made both Gail and Monica feel as if *she* had been silently favoured. It surprised each of them that this should matter so much and made for two very bad days. They did not even suggest practising their French.

Alfred sighed and took a luxurious drag on his cigarette. "Mozart's *Requiem* is the most popular concert of the year, next to the evening of music from American musicals." He drew the two tickets from the breast pocket of his jacket and placed them on the table. Was he trying to drive them crazy? They knew all about the concert; what they didn't know was who Alfred was taking. He looked first at Gail and then at Monica— warm, sympathetic looks— and then gave a Cheshire grin. "I only wish I have three tickets and we all can go," he shrugged. "But I think it is impossible for me to choose from two so very nice women. I think you must decide."

"What?" said Gail.

"I must be going to make the afternoon deliveries. Here, I leave the tickets with you"— he pushed them across the table. "You are friends, I know. You choose who is to go. Meet me here, at the Deux Garçons, ten minutes before the concert. We can walk from here. All right? I think this is the best way. The *most interesting* way. You are both so very nice."

Alfred rose from his chair, leaned over to kiss them twice, and started to whistle as he went out the doors. They heard the sound of his motor scooter putter up the Cours Mirabeau.

For some time Gail and Monica sat without speaking. The café had become noisy with customers and the waiters hurried past with full plates and bottles of wine. Finally Gail said, "Can you believe that?"

"He's going bald on top," Monica said. "That's why he wears that beret. I've decided who's going to the concert."

"Wait a minute— "

"Both of us. Alfred can stand in front of the Deux Garçons until dawn if he likes. Meanwhile, we'll be in the theatre listening to the *Requiem*. I don't think I've ever told you how much I love Mozart."

"*Moi aussi*," Gail said. "*J'aime Mozart.*"

And together they said: "It is very great and very sad."

And burst out laughing. So that they couldn't stop and had to gasp for air. So that they clutched each other by the shoulders. So that tears came to their eyes. So that, for the first time in six months, the waiters and the old women in fur collars stared at the two women who looked like sisters.

What is so beautiful about coffee in a cup? Why, on the eve of a new war, so terrible to contemplate, so unimaginable, why does this cup make the world smaller, more human?

The Boy Who Read *A Simple Heart*

AT THE AGE OF TWELVE I told my mother that some day I would be a great writer.

This is how it came about. One afternoon I wandered about the house in a state of pleasant and sleepy boredom. It was a school day but I had a mild cold and, exaggerating my symptoms, was permitted to stay in bed. When my mother left to do the shopping I got up and, still in my pyjamas, came down the staircase. In the library I began to look idly through my parents' books, most of which they both brought to the marriage and had added little to since.

I was more interested in climbing up the precarious face of the bookshelves. But one title caught my eye: *A Simple Heart* by G. Flaubert. Perhaps it was the green binding, or its wonderfully small size. I took the book upstairs and then, secretly under my covers, spent much of the next two days reading. It was a story about a servant like the woman who came to help my mother clean the chandelier. Also it was about a parrot. In the end, both the parrot and the woman died. Occasionally something struck me as funny and I laughed beneath my covers. But in the end it was sad. It was the best story I'd ever read.

On the third morning of this convalescence my mother brought me breakfast on a tray: oatmeal, toast and jam, orange slices, tea. I knew that this was the last morning that she'd let me stay in. While she sat with me I told her that one day I would write a story as fine as *A Simple Heart* by G. Flaubert. To my surprise her eyes widened, she hugged me, and telephoned my father. I had confirmed to them that I was special.

When I was sixteen I began writing stories. However, none of them pleased me. From the shelf I took down *A Simple Heart*, which I had not looked at since I was a child, although I believed that there was a unique relation between me and its author— a kind of secret mutual understanding. How little I had understood the first time! Now I could see that it was about love unrequited, for Félicité, the servant woman, is jilted by her man. After putting it down I felt highly agitated.

At the time I had a girlfriend from high school. In the basement of her parents' house I told her that I would one day write a story as great as *A Simple Heart* by Flaubert. She took me in her arms and for the first time we made love. The next day I attempted to fashion a story out of this event, but it came out badly and I threw it away. Evidently I was not ready.

At university I enroled in French literature. In my third year of study with only a little difficulty I managed

to read *A Simple Heart* in the original language of
Flaubert. How immature I had once been, I saw now,
and how inadequate is translation. The story was about
faithfulness and devotion— Félicité's devotion to her
mistress, Mme Aubain, and to young Virginie and
Victor. And clearly it was an allegory for the writer
himself and his devotion to his art. I felt choked with
emotion, for the story seemed to speak to me more
personally than ever.

At university I enroled in a course on creative
writing. The professor was a woman. In her office,
trembling, I told her that one day I would write a story
as great— or at least as moving— as *A Simple Heart*.
She smiled sadly, said that I had an admirable goal, and
invited me for dinner. We became lovers. At the end
of the year I wrote a story about us and handed it in as
my final assignment. My professor-lover gave the story
a mark of "average." She had been fair, as always. The
feeling had escaped the story, like a moth fluttering up
between one's fingers.

After graduation I obtained a job as an editor at a
firm publishing school textbooks. I believed this to be
a temporary position, and it was there that I worked
for almost thirty years, rising to the position of presi-
dent and surviving all purges, buy-outs, and other
financial storms. After I'd already risen to a senior
position we hired a young woman who had the

makings of a talented editor. One evening, over dinner in a restaurant, I told her that ever since I was a child I had wanted to write a story as fine as *A Simple Heart* by Flaubert, but that I was beginning to doubt whether I would ever finish a story that even satisfied some lesser standard. She said: Don't give up hope; remember that Flaubert wrote his story when he was an old man, full of maturity. And then she took my hand.

We married. Had children. My father died and then my mother. After the second funeral I came home and sank into a chair in my study. On the table was that first, green-covered copy of *A Simple Heart*, which I had taken from my mother's house. I picked it up and read it again. The story spoke to me of suffering, resignation, and death; and I wept noisily.

Our children have grown up and we have grown old. Our life together has been a good one. Not long ago I retired from the publishing firm, so that now I have time on my hands. After a few weeks of idleness in which I wandered about the house in my pyjamas as I once had as a child, a story began to form in my mind as if by a kind of divine grace. I walked around for several days in a spell. Finally, when my wife (who is ailing) was out visiting, I sat down at my desk and began to write. I wrote page after page, until it began to get dark. And then, as assuredly as it had begun, the story disintegrated. My pen skipped; I became unsure.

What I'd written on the previous pages suddenly seemed shallow and stilted, not at all what I had felt. I knew this was the last time, and I put the pen away.

That night, after my wife fell asleep, I took from the night-table where I now keep it, *A Simple Heart*. I began to read it again, perhaps also for the last time. It seemed to me about a servant, a parrot— I knew not what. I couldn't follow it, the words blurred. Putting it down, I turned out the light. In her sleep, my wife reached out for me. What I felt then I knew that I would never capture in words, and I lay down and stared into the darkness.

The drunk on the Rue de Buci who puts his too-firm arm around me and tells me to enjoy life. (After I've refused his request for change.) This is what I want to believe in: a city where the drunks are happy.

A Melancholy Bride

SOME PEOPLE— not many— come to a watershed in their lives. It divides what came before from what comes after. Martha's came at eleven thirty in the morning, on a Wednesday in January. But let us take a step backward.

She had spent the morning in the Louvre, standing before Corot's "The Bride." A small, almost miniature painting, it portrayed a young woman in three-quarter view, wearing a traditional bridal gown. The background had no detail, but was an eggshell hue crisscrossed with fine cracks. It was hung with the other Corots in a small room off the Grande Salle and Martha, standing a few feet back and just to one side, was often jostled by tourists as she balanced her notebook in one palm and wrote:

Figure presented directly, without adornment. Slightly artificial angularity, as if sculptural: the narrow face (colouring more grey than flesh tone), the lines around the almond eyes. Painted in the early 1840s, about the same time as several other studio portraits. Like them never exhibited during Corot's life. No doubt a genre figure for the artist, who never married.

Martha's black hair had grown long in the last three months and she left it wilder about her face, like the French. She wore a scarf, an old suede jacket, jeans, and pointed boots. She had no difficulty writing a description of the painting, commenting on technique, comparing it to the earlier Neo-classicists or the Impressionists who followed. What she failed to capture was how the painting affected her— its contagious melancholy. Was it the tilt of the figure's beautifully angular head, the plainness of the dress, the tones that seemed so sombre despite their lightness? Or perhaps the painting wasn't melancholy at all and Martha was infecting it with her own feeling. If so then the language of academic discourse was not merely inadequate; it was irrelevant. Because Martha herself was irrelevant.

After her legs began to ache from standing and her unhappiness soured to despair, she made her way through the Grande Galérie, down one of the palatial stairways, and out through the glass pyramid. It was sharply cold and, no longer wanting to think, she headed for the nearby café where she often went to finish up her notes. Inside, she sat at a table by the window where the winter light made her squint and opened her notebook. Not because she expected to write anything, but so as to appear to have a reason for being there.

Martha ordered tea. The theme of her dissertation had been crystal clear before she had left for Paris, had been wonderfully affirmed on her first visits to the Louvre, and from then on had begun to inexorably disintegrate. Now her working title, "A Century of French Portraiture: From Bourgeois Humanism to Pure Aestheticism," seemed a mere string of words. She was one-third the way through her nine-month grant and feared that if she stayed to the end she would come home with nothing at all. Should she return early then, to save her degree and herself?

The waiter brought the tea and Martha, feeling the cold through the window, wrapped her hands around the cup. Return early! When she had bragged to everyone she knew, had denigrated their home town for its complacent ignorance, its cultural backwardness, had told everyone how "spiritually hungry" she was for Paris. "I don't belong here, I'm different from everyone else, like a changeling," she had said to Gerry Mann, who had already asked her to marry him three times. "How can you be so satisfied here? It sickens me." At night in bed (she still lived in her parents' house, for economy's sake) she had imagined this new life unfolding around her, bringing a passionate sense of her own being.

This, however, was the reality: she did not have a single French friend, she was scared to death of her *concierge*, dining alone was becoming increasingly painful. At the Sorbonne, Professor Lefèbvre, to whom she had been given a letter of introduction, allowed her six minutes in his book-lined office. The Parisians were as indifferent to her as if she were a statue in the Touleries. No, they were worse than that, for at least they admired the statues, whereas toward her they were contemptuous. Just yesterday a man had sat beside her in a brasserie, his wire-haired dog curled up beside him. When Martha tried to pet the dog it bared its small teeth and lunged at her hand. The owner, a handsome and beautifully dressed man, proceeded to tell her off. Someone else would have given it right back to the man, but Martha apologized and spent the evening weeping in her room like an idiot.

She did manage to quieten herself by turning the incident into an amusing letter to Gerry Mann. What an unappealing irony that his letters, arriving every other day, should become events to look forward to. They were full of the most boring gossip from home, greetings from people she'd been only too glad to flee from, and maudlin recollections of their sexual relations. She even found comfort in his monotonous offers of marriage, and liked to read them while propped up in bed with a pastry in one hand.

Martha, looking at the pavement outside the window, said to herself: You can't be homesick for a place you despise. Or can you? It was a miserable thought, and she felt at her lowest and most vulnerable. At that moment she could have been easily seduced or converted to a religious cult.

Then came the watershed.

A fuss had begun in the street outside the window. A limousine had pulled against the curb and a group of men in morning dress were walking toward it, all speaking at once. From inside Martha couldn't hear them; they looked like figures in a silent movie, even in the stiff way they moved. Following them came women in silk dresses, rubbing their bare arms in the cold. One of the men opened the back door of the limousine and the whole crowd turned.

From somewhere (apparently a door next to the café) emerged a figure in a white gown. A small woman scurried behind, holding up the train. The others opened a passage so the figure could step to the door of the limousine. First the small woman pulled the train into the car and then the bride, turning around, began to ease herself in. For a moment Martha saw only the veil pinned into her heavy red hair, but then her face came up. It was a round face, generously freckled. The bride seemed to catch her reflection in the window— or did she see Martha looking at her?— for she hesitated. The concentration on her face broke and she laughed, not daintily, but in an open, healthy, and almost brash way.

The door of the limousine closed, there was a bustle of movement, and the procession was gone.

Martha touched her cup; the tea was cold. She ordered another from the passing waiter and drank it hot. Then she opened her notebook and wrote:

For better or worse, no one has a firmer place in this world than a bride. But that lasts for a single day, and then what? Corot painted his with tenderness but that's not much to live on. He couldn't understand her as a woman does— as I do. I know more than Corot, more than Professor Lefèbvre, more than Gerry Mann!

Martha finished her tea. She paid the bill and left, stepping into a new, a transformed Paris. Six months later she left the city with the greatest regret. But every so often afterwards— for example, when she stood before her own students for the first time, and whenever she herself walked down an aisle— she felt that she was accompanied by her two brides, one melancholy and the other laughing.

You wake me: an anti-war march on Boulevard St. Germain. The sound of chanting through the window as we pull our clothes onto our damp bodies. But by the time we reach the street the march has passed.

Domesticity

IT RAINED the two days we spent in Arles, from the moment we stepped off the train. We had no hotel reservation— Sarah insisted that reservations took the adventure out of travel— and so we had to tramp with our baggage up from the station along the brown Rhone and into the streets of the town. I held an umbrella over my head as my bag bumped against my legs, but Sarah, carrying her knapsack, went bareheaded, her blond hair drenched and clinging to her face. She enjoyed getting soaked.

We found a two-star hotel (that was one of our compromises; I would have preferred more comforts) and hung up our wet clothes. I wanted to stay in and listen to the rain or read my book on the decline of American power, but Sarah couldn't wait to see the theatre. At this point in the trip (we'd already been to sites in Greece and Italy) her enthusiasm for ancient architecture was, if anything, even more keen and I knew it would be a mistake to complain.

In the middle of the afternoon the town was shut up for lunch. The streets were so impossibly narrow that when a car came by we had to press ourselves against the stone wall. Although Sarah was only five

years younger than I, we seemed of different generations. She looked like the student she was, with a
bandanna in her hair, her jeans and runners. Sarah's
PhD was in a joint architecture and theatre history
program of her own devising and for her research we
had visited more than a dozen Greek and Roman
theatres where she had taken photographs and mea-
surements. She even had special authority (the papers
had taken months to acquire) to walk where tourists
weren't permitted.

The Roman theatre at Arles was better preserved
than most. It stood just behind the arena which looked
like a smaller version of the Colosseum in Rome, but
which Sarah hardly glanced at. Arenas were for spec-
tacles, not drama, and she considered them as interesting as hockey rinks. She showed our pass to the woman
who sold tickets and walked up to the theatre, a rising
half-circle of stone seats facing a modern wooden stage
used for the annual summer festival. Of the architec-
tural structure that had once formed the backdrop for
the plays, two columns remained, the pink marble
stained from the rain. Sarah stood for almost an hour
on the muddy ground in a kind of rapture while the
ticket seller sat under a broken arch, staring at us as she
cracked pecans in her lap.

That night we ate in the restaurant adjacent to the
hotel, a long silent meal in which we merely watched

the level of the wine descend in the bottle. We were both angry, I because my new Italian shoes were stained (I'd have to find a bottle of vinegar to clean them) and she because my "sulking," as she called it, had almost spoiled her first view of the theatre. I knew what Sarah thought; that I shouldn't have bought the shoes, or brought with me the jacket and tie that I always wore at dinner. But I believed that Europeans gave better service to foreigners who weren't dressed like bums.

Taking these weeks off to travel had been difficult; perhaps I'd even jeopardized my future with the firm. But I had come for Sarah's sake, to prove to her that she was more important than my work. The evening in her apartment when I told her I could go she threw her arms around me and took me straight to bed. But underneath this generosity was the fear of letting Sarah go without me.

The rain continued and after dinner we returned to our room. Sarah put on the big shirt she slept in and sprawled onto the bed, recording in a book her impressions of the site. Without saying anything I took from her knapsack the bag she used for laundry and proceeded to wash our socks and underwear in the corner sink. I had brought a small container of soap powder for this purpose and methodically rinsed each item before draping it on the warm radiator. By some unspoken agreement these small domestic acts had become my responsibility; Sarah had no feel for them and would have been happy wearing dirty things. But the truth was that washing in the sink at the end of the day soothed me in a way that nothing else did since we had left. At the beginning, when we were still in Greece, Sarah had teased me, saying that she would buy me an apron trimmed with lace. I hadn't minded really, but somewhere along the way she dropped the joke.

"I cannot believe how repressed you are," she said without looking up from her notebook. She stretched out her arm in a half-hearted attempt to drop her cigarette ash on the floor rather than the bed. "You're a prisoner of your own little obsessions."

"I'm not the only one with obsessions," I said. "It's just that yours are the opposite of mine. You have a compulsive need to make a mess."

"You're right, we never had a single thing in common, right from the beginning."

"Please, Sarah, not again."

"I don't care. I think we should split up— we're just too different. All we ever do is drive each other crazy. I think we'd be happier if we went our separate ways."

"That isn't true."

She looked up. We both had tears in our eyes. We met in the middle of the room and held each other. "I didn't mean it," she said. "I'm sorry. It's the rain, that's all."

But I was afraid that she did mean it. The next morning I awoke with a start and reached over to feel her warm shoulder. I had been sure that she wouldn't be there beside me.

In season, the guidebooks say, Arles is a pretty town, overgrown with vines, and the cafés crowded on the Boulevard des Lices. But in winter it was easy to see why Gauguin and Van Gogh had become so bitter and despondent here. As we walked, the matronly women in the shops stared suspiciously at us through their windows. In the empty cafés American pop music played from jukeboxes. Drenched with rain, we trudged through the town to the Alyscamps, the old cemetery whose ornate sarcophagi had long been moved elsewhere, and then took shelter in the inevitable museum named after the local Romantic artist. But for some reason everything began to seem funny. We laughed at paintings until we ached and the guard asked us to leave; we crooned "Singin' in the Rain" as we splashed through puddles; we played video games in a sour-smelling bar while young men frowned at Sarah. In the late afternoon we returned to the hotel, chilled to the bone, pulled off our clothes, and got into the icy bed. Our bodies seemed more real to each other than ever before— the only living, warm things in this dreary town.

Only at dinner time did we get up again. Sarah overturned her knapsack in a search for dry clothes. "Damn," she said. "My second pair of jeans has a rip in it."

"Where?"

"Here, in the crotch."

"That's not a rip, they're just worn out. I did suggest you buy a new pair for the trip."

"Is this a speech? Because if it is I'll take notes."

"Maybe you could use one," I said.

She tossed the jeans onto the floor. I picked them up, fished out my portable sewing kit, and sat down at the table by the window. With each careful stitch I drew I could feel Sarah's hatred for me grow. After the last, I folded the jeans and placed them on the bed. She snatched them up to pull them on, grabbed her coat and slammed the door behind her. From the window I could see her enter the street and pause for a small police car to go by before running down the cobblestones. After she turned the corner I picked up my book and sat down again.

When I next looked up the street had turned dark, although the steady sound of rain on the shutters hadn't changed. In my jacket and tie I went down to the restaurant for dinner.

"*Vous attendez Madame?*" the owner asked me.

"*Non,*" I said.

I ate slowly and drank a bottle of wine, not the local kind that Sarah claimed had more character, but an eight-year-old Burgundy. When I finally got up I was surprised to find myself unsteady on my feet. Outside, the rain had stopped. Everything was wet; the arches and rails overhead dripped steadily. I walked down the inclining street, unsure of the direction that I was heading. The town was deserted. I reached a poorly lit square from where I could see the moon, cold and white. It illuminated the shape of the arena and beside it the two columns of the theatre. When I got near I saw Sarah standing by the iron gate. She didn't appear surprised to see me, but said,

"The gate's locked at night."

"We can climb it," I said.

She looked at me. "That's illegal. Someone will see us."

"Not over there, beside the trees."

We slipped in between the branches and the fence and I gave Sarah a boost. I followed, slipping once so that an iron point pressed against my side. In the moonlight the theatre looked more intimate. Sarah climbed onto the stage while I walked up the rising tiers of seats. It seemed to take a long time to reach the top. Down below Sarah stood on the stage, stretched out her arms, and began to recite something in Greek, the words rising clearly. For the first time this was more than just a ruin to me. Once people had filled these seats, eager for tragedy. Sarah finished her speech and as I clapped she took a bow. Then she dropped down from the stage and started to walk up the tiers toward me.

When she got to the top she stood beside me and looked at the theatre below as I looked at her face. A phrase came into my head and I said it aloud: "Washed in moonlight." Sarah didn't look at me but she smiled. I saw she was shivering, so I put my arm around her and we walked down together. And I knew she wouldn't leave me. Not in Arles.

Miklós Radnóti, "drunk from writing poems,"
watched the dawn rise over the city and listened to
the cats mating on the roof. Paris, how many souls
have loved you, but loved somewhere else more
and so returned home again? Radnóti went back to
Hungary to die in a mass grave, his pockets stuffed
with poems.

But Miklós, that caressing sky above is your sky,
so you must still be here...

Woodenheads

I AM A PUPPETEER. It is an occupation that has run in my family for generations and it is an honourable one, or at least it used to be. More than once I have had to assert that puppetry is an art with a venerable tradition. It has its great artists and its great history, recorded in books now difficult to come by.

As a puppeteer I work alone. The form that I practise is of the purest kind. My stage I carry on my back: collapsed, it appears somewhat like a deck chair, but in a few moments its wood and canvas is transformed into a theatre promising as much as any theatre can. My puppets hang upside down from my wide leather belt, bouncing lifelessly as I walk through one of the city's parks, proclaiming the start of a show. I wear a cloth hat with six points, but otherwise dress as a workman. In cold weather I wear a sweater beneath my jacket and a good pair of longjohns. Inevitably, as my voice rings out, the children begin to run toward me, followed in a more leisurely fashion by their parents. From the eye of a bird this would look like the stars moving toward their sun; that's what I have imagined in my less humble moments.

While the plays that I perform change, the setting and characters do not. They have been used by my family for generations and I have felt no need to alter them. The painted backdrop of the stage shows the main square of the Town of Woodenheads. Its inhabitants are the Boy, the Tramp, the Policeman, the Buxom Young Wench, the Old Crone, and the Dog. Over the years I have worn out many puppets, but their faces remain the same— unsmiling, sharp-featured, slightly grotesque. I make them in the evenings, working slowly with blocks of wood, scraps of material, wire and paint. Sometimes over a beer in the tavern the men I've known all my life will urge me to bring my shows up to date. I would do much better, they say, if my puppets were superheroes, pop singers, film stars. I don't even answer, and why should I?

This winter I performed a play called *The Dog Eats the Laundry*. I write my plays— or rather I make them up, for nothing is ever written down— while working on the puppets, or freshening up the stage with new paint. The play, as simple as all the others, shows the townspeople as dunces, incapable of solving the simplest dilemma. In this play the Dog eats the laundry that the Old Crone has hung up to dry. The Old Crone accuses everyone of stealing her underthings and there is much shouting, tears, faints. The foolishness of the townspeople makes things right again, as the Policeman, pulling on the Dog's tongue to stop its barking, accidently pulls the laundry from its mouth, still on the line.

Sunday has always been the best day for my work, when families are together and parents are anxious for ways to occupy their children. But times have changed. Children are now allowed to run about on their own, or stay inside and play with their computers. While in the past I was never without some fear of hard times one or two months down the road, life has become more precarious. To keep body and soul together I must perform six shows every Sunday instead of four, moving each week to a different park. And I'm older now; at the end of the day my feet throb and my voice is hoarse.

This Sunday I had a particularly bad day. In the morning it was cold and threatened rain. The few children and adults who answered my call looked restless before I even began. The mere entrance of each character did not please as usual, and I had to double my efforts, exaggerating the movements of the puppets beyond what I believed to be artistic. During one performance a child yelled out the ending before it happened. The money dropped into the hat afterwards was hardly enough for a meal.

For the afternoon I decided to try another park. I walked down the path, calling with a forced joviality, my breath visible in the air. The children came, but instead of running eagerly, they made their way slowly, as if already bored. The parents who followed looked cold and grim as they arranged themselves in a semi-circle before the stage.

"And now," I pronounced in the voice of a master of ceremonies, "*The Dog Eats the Laundry.*"

"But we've already seen that one," a child moaned.

"Yes," an adult followed, "you were here only two weeks ago."

Apparently I had forgotten. "Well then," I announced, "how about *The Policeman Makes an Arrest.*"

"We've seen that one too!"

Those on the edge of the circle began to turn away. "Wait," I shouted, unable to hide the desperation in my voice. "I will perform a new play, never seen before."

"That's better," someone said, there was scattered laughter, and they settled down again.

"It is called *The Tramp Comes to Woodenheads Town.*"

I began the play with only the sketchiest notion of a story. The Tramp arrived in town, hungry and footsore, and put down his bundle. He sang a sentimental little tune about the warmth of his mother's bed. Picking up his bundle again, he saw the Old Crone through her kitchen window, baking bread. But when he asked her for a loaf she closed the shutters in his face.

"Good," someone called out from the audience. "There are too many of these derelicts around nowadays."

Next the Tramp saw the Buxom Young Wench, mixing a stew in a great pot. But when he asked her for a bowl she called him "Eyesore" and "Droop-Ass" and threatened him with her wooden spoon.

"That's it," someone else shouted. "Why should he live on our backs? We pay enough as it is."

The Tramp, more hungry than before, sat down on a step to rest. He recited a nonsense rhyme about how sitting at a window and looking down at the street was so much more pleasant than sitting in the street and looking up at a window. When the Policeman came by he said, "Who gave you permission to sit on the step of the Town Hall?" and threatened to put him in jail. So the Tramp moved on, only to meet the Boy, whose Dog began to growl. Each time the audience, children and adults alike, called out their approval. Despite the cold I began to sweat beneath my clothes, for I had planned for the tramp to trick the townspeople during the afternoon market. Angered by his taunts of stinginess, they were to throw vegetables at him, which he would catch in his open bundle. But during the market scene the audience saw what I was up to and began to shout derisively. And then, as if by divine grace, came a moment of inspiration.

At the last second the Dog bounded up to the Tramp and tore the bundle from his hands, exposing the scheme. The townspeople gathered round and beat him, the Old Crone with her rolling pin, the Buxom Young Wench with her spoon, the Policeman with his club, the Boy with his leash. Only the Policeman paused for a moment, to bestow a kiss on the Buxom Young Wench's rosy bosom.

There was much applause and the hat filled with coins and even bills.

I did not perform another show that afternoon, but instead went to a restaurant and had a long meal, with a decent bottle of wine, and afterwards, brandy. For it is not often that a person's efforts are truly appreciated, and he ought to enjoy the moment when it comes. What's more, I knew that I had a play to sustain me for some months.

As to whether the townspeople beat the poor Tramp to death, or merely taught him a lesson, I left that up to the imagination of the audience. A detail such as that is what separates the mere journeyman from the artist.

The white-haired proprietress makes a flourish of pouring the wine; watered down, but we appreciate the gesture just the same. Her husband winds the player piano and sings Charles Aznavour ballads. Instead of listening, I think of the elderly woman who placed roses at the Mémorial de la Déportation behind Notre-Dame. She carried her lapdog in a large handbag.

Are They Really Cézanne's Apples?

STEVE AND ARLENE FISK ran into Shoshana and David
Zeligman on the grounds of Cézanne's studio. Steve
and Arlene had been laughing at that moment, while
Shoshana and David were engrossed in a conversation.
When the couples saw each other they simply stopped.
It was a late August day and hot. The paths were dusty,
the grass and plane trees drained of colour by the
Provençal sun. The women made little whoops of joy
while the men shook hands vigorously. And then Steve
and Shoshana hugged; after all, they'd been camp
counsellors together ten years ago. There was a burst
of conversation— a comparison of itineries— followed
by awkward silence.

A passing train of Japanese tourists, wearing ties and
carrying video recorders, gave the Fisks and the
Zeligmans something to smile at together. Steve said,
"Have you been inside the studio yet? We're just
going."

"No, we just arrived," Shoshana said, perhaps too
enthusiastically, for she added, "but maybe David
wants to look around the grounds first."

"You mean I get to choose?" David joked. Shoshana
looked surprised at him.

"We're not planning to stay very long," Arlene said. "We haven't had lunch yet."

"What a great idea," Steve said, taking her hand. "We can all go to lunch together." Arlene smiled, but she dropped Steve's hand.

"That'll be a relief," Shoshana said. "We haven't spoken English to anyone but each other for two weeks, have we, David?"

"Are we going in or aren't we?" David said.

Shoshana took him by the arm. "Suddenly my husband's the big art lover."

AS IT TURNED OUT, the studio did not take more than a few minutes to view. The dour woman who took their tickets told them that Cézanne had used the studio until his death in 1906 and that all the objects were "*originale.*" The two couples stood in the centre of the room, looking at the tall north windows, the straw-backed chair, the dried up pallet and wine bottles covered in dust.

"Just imagine," said Shoshana. "Those are the apples that Cézanne painted. It's amazing."

They looked down at three wrinkled apples in a wooden bowl. David said, "Come on, Shoshana. Are they really Cézanne's apples? I don't see how they can be that old. It must be a con."

"But the woman said so," Steve offered.

"You're so sweet when you're being naive," Arlene said and squeezed his chin as if he were a child.

Just then the Japanese tourists filed in and the studio was filled with the whirr of cameras.

The restaurant they chose for lunch was near to Shoshana and David's hotel on the Place du General De Gaulle. Arlene looked displeased as soon as they were handed menus: she and Steve, she told them, preferred the less expensive places that were frequented by locals. "Our hotel is near the train station. It's absolutely quaint, not even an elevator. At night you can hear the trains whistle."

The men were allowed to scrutinize the wine bill. They kept alternating suggestions, moving further down the list until they had no choice but to order champagne. The cork was popped, a toast was made by Steve ("To unexpected meetings..."), and the meal that followed passed in pleasurable chatter. Afterwards they each amusingly accused the others of drinking all the champagne.

When the coffee came Arlene said, "To me Cézanne is only a *technically* interesting painter. For content he doesn't compare to either Gauguin or Van Gogh."

"Do you think so, honey?" Steve said. "I don't know. I see tremendous passion in those apples and oranges."

"Me too," Shoshana nodded. "It's the intensity, the purity. They move me in a way I can hardly describe."

"Since when?" David said. "I thought you liked Picasso."

"Sweetheart, it's possible to like more than one painter."

"Actually," Steve tapped his spoon energetically on the table, "Picasso learned a hell of a lot from Cézanne. That's probably what Shoshana sees."

"How do you know what Shoshana sees?" Arlene said. "Just because you *shtupped* her one night in an empty cabin?"

"Yeah, and on the floor yet," David said.

Shoshana said quietly: "We had a blanket."

"And a pillow," Steve added.

"Are you going to paint a picture, for Christ's sake?" David said with disgust.

"You were the one who wanted to know about my past," Shoshana said. "You got off on it."

"Oh, right," was all he could say. "I'm getting out of here."

David threw down his napkin, noisily pushed back his chair, and squeezed his way between the tables.

"Great," said Steve. "He sticks me with the bill."

"That's all you talk about," Arlene said. "Saving money. If you weren't so cheap we'd have a damn shower in our room."

She threw down her napkin and went out.

Steve and Shoshana looked down into their cups. The sound of French voices, lulled for a moment, rose around them. Steve rocked his cup in its saucer, rubbed his forehead, and said: "I guess we better go after them."

"Yes," Shoshana said. They looked at one another. "But not yet."

"No," Steve smiled. "Not yet."

War has started; the man with the bad leg told me. How strange to be in this train, travelling through the French countryside, while somewhere bombs are falling through the sky.

Train Stations Are Beautiful

FRENCH TRAIN STATIONS are beautiful. Even the ordinary ones, in ordinary towns. Maybe that's just the way they look to us, because of the romantic ideas we have on holiday. I suppose it's ironic that Arthur died right on the platform, in such an exquisite spot. It was our second trip to France. The first had been our honeymoon, forty-one years before.

Arthur liked to be a little daring in our travels, and he chose Foix over nearby Carcassonne. We waited at the exit door of the train as it pulled into the station, stopping and starting a few times. After Paris (it's so smoggy there now, all those tour buses) the air was fresh. The platform was open and I could see a few low hills, brown and green, in the distance, and it was very quiet. Arthur pulled the bags down from the train himself. Then he got out the Michelin to check the hotel's name for the third time, he was obsessive like that. He wanted the trip to be perfect. For example, when we opened the door of the hotel room in Paris there were roses waiting on the table. So he opened the guidebook, made a noise, and fell down.

Arthur was a specialist in transportation law. It wasn't the most lucrative field, but he made a good living. He knew his area inside and out, especially the laws pertaining to shipping by sea, and he tended to give advice on the conservative side. He thought that a sensible practice, but it was also his nature. One day Arthur received a special delivery letter from the French Institute, asking him to give a paper at a conference on the law of the sea. Experts from all over the world would be there, even Eastern Europe. Arthur tried not to show it but he was very pleased. It isn't often that a man who doesn't blow his own horn gets recognized. So we decided to make it a holiday, a week in Paris and then another ten days travelling to the south.

Arthur spent over three months working on that paper. At night, in bed while we had our tea and biscuits (a ritual left from when the children were small) he would talk about it. The paper had to do with the impact of *Glasnost* on shipping. I didn't understand all the legal technicalities, but I got the gist of it. Arthur liked trying out his ideas on me and said that my response helped him to "sharpen" them. Maybe he was trying to flatter me, because I only have a grade ten education. I always worried about showing my ignorance around Arthur's colleagues and their wives, but he respected my judgment, I know that. It was one of the things I loved about him.

Once Arthur had the paper pretty well written, he spent quite a lot of time on the ending. He wanted to go beyond the legal talk of the rest of the paper, to rise into the world of people. Maybe it showed the emotional streak in him. Finally one night he came up from the basement and read it to me in bed. I thought it was as beautiful as poetry.

The ending of the Cold War will do more than remove many of the longstanding barriers to shipping trade. It will make the ocean smaller, so that those of us in the West and those in the East will be able to reach across and shake hands.

The conference lasted three days and Arthur gave his paper on the last afternoon. The audience wasn't as large as I had pictured— only about sixty or so— but they listened very attentively and when he was finished applauded warmly. I think it was the ending that did it. Arthur looked out over his glasses and smiled.

The conference ended with a dinner and afterwards ballroom dancing. Everyone was very friendly, but the truth is I only had eyes for Arthur. I had thought that stuff about a second honeymoon was nonsense, but that was how we felt. He took me in his arms and we danced. Arthur was always a better dancer than I was, and when he dipped me I felt lightheaded. He looked at me with passion and I wasn't frightened as I had been forty-one years ago.

The day before we left Paris, Arthur started to feel strange. I thought it was the excitement of the conference catching up to him, and also the heavy meals. He had a bad night and was irritable in the morning. The train ride was surprisingly hard on him. He wouldn't look at me or touch me, but kept checking his watch, getting out of his seat, pacing the corridor. He panicked when we had to change trains and at first refused to get off. In a voice that people could hear he called me a "stupid woman."

But then, as we got closer to Foix, he became calm. He called me over and I stood with him by the window to watch the countryside go by. He didn't seem to remember what he'd said to me. Instead, he talked about buying a cottage here and coming every summer— just a daydream, I knew, but lovely to hear anyway.

I don't want to describe what happened at the station. Nobody spoke English and it took half an hour to get an ambulance. But Arthur was already dead. I don't remember how I got to the hotel, or telephoned Noah in Boston. He flew over that night. All that French red tape, the piles of documents to fill in order to bring Arthur back home. I kept saying that a Jew must be buried immediately. That I remember.

At the funeral Rabbi Perl bent over his prayer book and the men took turns tossing earth onto the casket.

Afterwards the house filled with people. Somehow food appeared on the dining room table and there was always a *minyan* for prayer. Then the people stopped coming and my sons and daughter took their families home. Friends invited me for dinner, but I didn't go. For the first time I started thinking about how many people I was really close to. When I did see people I only wanted to talk about Arthur, that was the stage I was in after the shock, as if he was just taking a nap on the sofa. And then suddenly I didn't even want to talk about Arthur any more and had nothing to say at all.

So I stayed at home. It was surprising how much less the telephone rang. The afternoon that I decided to clean out all the cupboards was the time I first started drinking. We had liquor in the cabinet for guests; I began with the sweet liqueurs and went on to the bottles of wine, the bourbon, the vodka, and then the scotch. One afternoon Marilyn telephoned and listened to me slur my words. It wasn't long after that she asked me to move in with them. As she insisted I flew out to Vancouver and spent two weeks, sleeping in one of the kid's rooms while they doubled up. Don't get me wrong, they treated me like a queen, but the truth is my daughter gets on my nerves. It was a relief to come back.

I stopped drinking because the cabinet was empty and I was too ashamed of what Arthur would have said to go to the liquor store. That's when I started joining things. The bridge club. A course on Greek pottery. I always liked going to the theatre, but Arthur and I had made it only to the big shows at the Royal Alex— *Les Miz* was the last we saw together. Now I started going to the small theatres. It was quite exciting, I was only sorry that there was nobody to talk about the plays with afterward. One night I even saw *Waiting for Godot*. It made perfect sense to me.

That's how I met Henry. I had bought a coffee during intermission and he was holding the cream and offered to pour for me. Henry's a widower, twelve years on now. He was an actor for years, mostly in television commercials. He made a bare living but he has a pension now and lives in an apartment in Bathurst Manor. He still acts in amateur productions at the Jewish Y. Henry and I became theatre companions. It's much nicer to have somebody to go with and then to sit in a booth at Shopsy's and talk. Although he's an actor, Henry's taste is much more "mainstream" than mine. He thinks I'm Bohemian, especially when I wear one of my silk scarves around my neck. Next month he's in a production of *Guys and Dolls*.

A while ago I took Arthur's paper, the one he gave at the conference, and had a calligrapher write it out on sheets of handmade paper. Then I had it bound in leather, with the title in gold letters. It sits on the glass table in the living room. The other afternoon Henry read it and said that Arthur was a very intelligent man. If you want to know the truth, I don't think Henry understood a word of it. But he asked if he could read it out loud to me and I said yes. It didn't sound anything like Arthur's measured voice; Henry declaimed it, like he was playing Marc Antony. But I liked listening anyway, and I waited for the wonderful finish about the East and West. Henry stretched out his hand to an invisible partner as he read. He must not ever have been much of an actor. But I cried anyway, and then Henry and I walked up the stairs, me first and he following.

The woman in owl glasses turns out to be a Mormon missionary from Minnesota. She has been sent here (with no knowledge of the language) to knock on doors and convert the French nation. Forbidden to read newspapers, she has no idea a war is on. But she has been instructed not to attempt to convert any Arabs.

You'll Be Glad to Know

I HAVE NOTHING TO WRITE, I don't know why I'm even trying except that your father won't stop pestering me. What could I possibly have to say that would interest you? After all, it's from here that you want to get away.

You've written three letters. In one week! You have so much to say, that's certainly clear. But why shouldn't you? A new environment, you're young, it's easy to be stimulated and even excited about the future. Your father says to me, "Write back something cheerful." That's easy for a man who feels nothing more, but what's a matter of choice for him is impossible for me, I'm just not the sort. And as I too want only for you to be happy I think it's better not to write, not a single word.

But every morning your father says, "For God's sake when are you going to answer? He's waiting for a letter, he thinks you're angry." Well, I don't want you to think I'm angry and so I write. See— I'm writing. Even if this isn't the sort of easy chit-chat your father can produce in his sleep. Everybody has always liked your father, he's amusing, a good sport— in fact I'm envied by quite a few women at the club, you should just hear them in the locker room, you'd be proud of your father— or more likely you'd blush. They stand naked under the showers and it's shocking, the kind of language they use. Well, I haven't disillusioned them and I won't complain to you either, that would be simply unnatural, and besides you're having too good a time to care.

When I sat down I tried to remember the last time I wrote a letter. Not bills or a new year's card, but a real letter. Who do I have to write to? Once I had friends, good, close friends, but that was before your father came along and wanted me all to himself. Of course he denies this (if it's wrong to be so honest, I'm not the kind who can keep such things to herself and I don't regret it) but men have an extraordinary capacity to forget, it's a kind of gift. Yes, your father has forgotten a great deal, but I remember, not because I want to but because I have no choice. His gift, my curse.

Perhaps you've already managed to develop this gift yourself. Yes, I'm sure you have. Anyway, why should you have worries? You're at the stage when even troubles are pleasures. See, I remember. Oh yes, I was your age once too. There isn't a thing you are feeling that I myself haven't felt deeply and intensely, even blindingly. I mean nothing by saying it, I have no intention of belittling your own experience, it's simply a fact.

This from your letters: the lake is pretty, there is a *confiserie* in the town, your teachers are demanding but kind. I admit it then, your father was right to send you and I was wrong. I had my fears, but if so it was your welfare I was thinking about— that I've always put first. And who is to say that those fears won't still be justified? You are a sensitive boy and (it's true whether or not you're willing to admit it) delicate. I am afraid for you. And the plain fact is you've never been good at making friends. Was it wrong for me not to want you to get hurt? Of course, there was a time when you considered me your friend, or has the gift you've inherited from your father allowed you to forget that already? Think of all the games we played! I always made time, no matter how busy with adult duties. We spent hours together, I wasn't afraid to get down on my knees. Why should I wish to send you away knowing that you would sob every night into your pillow and wish you were home?

And you did sob once, your first night, you admit that in your first letter. True, you refer to it briefly and with dismissal, but it's not hard for me who knows you so well to imagine the truth: hours and hours of stifled weeping and loneliness. The second night you didn't cry, or so you say. And by the third letter you already have three friends!

Of course I am as thrilled for you as I am surprised, but that doesn't mean I approve of your allowing them to convince you to play soccer. To think how hard I struggled to have you exempted from gym classes at school, how you begged me and I had to speak to the nurse three times and get a letter from Doctor Lask. Apparently that was all unnecessary, you're actually as strong as a dockworker and your nights of wheezing from asthma are in the past. Excuse me if I can't quite believe it. No doubt your arms and legs are already scratched and bruised. There was a time when you would come to me with every hurt, every injury, and insist I kiss it better. Now I picture you, after one of your glorious soccer victories, flat on your back and gasping for breath. That's the nightmare your letters have left me with.

The food, you say, isn't very good. I don't know what you expected.

You see, all I can do is respond to your letters, I have nothing to say about myself. Your father— about him, at least, there is something to write. He has a life outside this house, even if what he calls "healthy male companionship" I call sickness. "Keep yourself busy," he tells me, "do something for distraction." Distraction that he doesn't need, he already has enough. But I've taken his advice, you'll be glad to know I'm not stubborn or deliberately morose. My little project is to redecorate your room, from top to bottom. Right now it is stripped bare and when you do finally come home you won't recognize it.

Of course if I had a genuine husband I wouldn't need to be occupied. About this, though, you are hardly the person to act as confessor. Everyone agrees that there are certain things a child should be kept in the dark about and I absolutely concur. My role is to give, not to take. It's better for you to believe that your father and I are having a delirious time while you're gone, a second honeymoon. If there was a time when he used to leave the office early, so eager was he to see me, and I would wait for him, listening for the sound of the door— that belongs to a different era, a different life.

Believe me, I want you to be independent, I encourage it, and I'm glad you are having what you call your "adventure." Only one small word of advice, and not one that encroaches on your freedom. That is to beware this "Rose-Anne" you mention in your last letter, not even in the body of the letter but in the "P.S." First of all, since when have you decided that blond hair is pretty? Perhaps you're unaware that it signifies stupidity. And second, it was my impression from the brochures that male and female study halls were separate. As far as I recall, you never needed assistance on algebra before. If you do need help ask your teacher. It can be dangerous to learn from those with false ideas.

So you see that I have proven what I said, that I have nothing to write and am just filling empty space. It's time to close the envelope, your father will be home soon, no doubt with several new jokes to tell and smelling of cigars. I hear the door now; my heart jumps, for I imagine it is you, rushing in to see me. Remember, if you're not happy don't hide it, there is no shame, we would welcome you home with open arms. Write often and tell everything, above all enjoy yourself. Nobody prays for your happiness more than I do.

The Etruscan sarcophagus in the Louvre, of baked red clay. On the lid a sculpture of the married couple lying side by side, she in front and his arm around her, the two smiling as if they shared a secret.

In bed, we position our naked selves in just the same way. Our laughter suddenly turns solemn.

Baa Baa Black Sheep

I DIDN'T SEE MY BROTHER before he died. Hadn't seen him for eight years, or any of my family. It was weeks before the letter, shunting from address to address, found me. After I read the letter I picked up the telephone and booked an airline ticket. I wasn't sure why. After all, it was too late.

My brother's wife didn't meet me at the airport because she didn't know I was coming. When Maureen opened the door I was standing with an overnight bag in one hand and an overcoat draped on my arm. At first she didn't recognize me because of the beard. It took me a moment to realize that— I'd begun to grow the beard the day I'd left. Now there was grey in my hair, at the sides, and in my beard. "Joshua," she said when she realized who I was and threw her thin arms around my shoulders. She started to cry.

My brother was forty-eight when he died, twelve years older than me. Maureen was his second wife; the three children by his first were already working or in university. She led me into the house, taking my bag and coat, insisting I stay in the guest room.

"How long will you be here? Have you come back for good?" she asked.

I intended to stay only a week. But I said, "A while." A sound came from another room. "Wait here a minute," she said and went out. I looked about the room, but nothing was familiar, not the furniture or the prints on the walls from American museums. The house was one of a new row of three in an otherwise old neighbourhood and the things in the room didn't look quite as if they belonged. The bay window had a view of the street. No cars, just dry grass and evenly spaced young trees tied to metal supports.

Maureen came in holding the hand of a little boy. He looked about two, in overalls and runners, his hair cut straight over his eyes.

"Jeremy," Maureen said, "this is your Uncle Joshua."

I crouched down. "Hi, Jeremy," I said and waved my fingers. He looked straight into my eyes. His were hazel, like my brother's had been. He looked identical to old baby pictures of Edward. He kept hold of his mother's hand, narrowing his eyes. His mouth turned down and as he turned to her, holding up his arms to be held, he started to cry.

"It's the beard," Maureen said apologetically. "He's always been afraid of men with beards, I don't know why. Come here," she cooed, hefting him into her arms. Jeremy buried his face in her shoulder. Then he turned his head to look at me, wailed even louder, and turned back.

"Maybe he'll get used to me," I said.

But he wouldn't. Maureen made us dinner and afterwards we sat over coffee in the living room. All evening Jeremy kept away from me, near his mother. Even when he played with his miniature cars he stretched out one stockinged foot to brush against her. Maureen and I talked about Edward, how he had just begun to get back on his feet financially, how happy he had been as a father again. "He talked about you all the time," she said, "as if he had just seen you the other day. At night he would read to Jeremy and then tell stories about things you two used to do as kids. Jeremy couldn't have understood, but he would sit quietly in bed and listen. Eddy never said, but I think he always hoped you would show up one day."

I looked into my cup. "This is good coffee," I said.

"Where Daddy?" Jeremy said without looking up from his cars. Maureen sighed. "What am I supposed to say?" she asked.

I crouched down and held out my arms. "Come here, Jeremy," I said and smiled.

"No." He held a small firetruck in his hand. I thought he might fling it. "I don't like you. Bad. The story man."

"What does he mean?" I said.

"I don't know. Maybe there was an evil person with a beard in one of the stories Eddy read to him. Let's go," she said, picking him up. "It's time for beddy-bye. Say goodnight to Uncle Joshua."

"You go away," he said.

IN THE MORNING I shaved off my beard. First I trimmed off as much as possible using a pair of scissors from a drawer in the kitchen. Then I used my razor, slowly and painfully, cutting the skin in several places. I had a hard time stopping the blood. My face didn't look like my brother's; I resembled the other side of the family. After I cleaned the sink I went into the kitchen where Jeremy sat in his high chair and Maureen held a spoon in the air.

They both looked at me. "Daddy," said Jeremy.

"No," said Maureen. "That's Uncle Joshua."

"Unk Jesh," he said.

While Maureen made me scrambled eggs for breakfast Jeremy let me feed him. "That's good, isn't it," I said, slipping another spoonful into his mouth. "You're hungry this morning, Jeremy."

"He's always hungry," Maureen laughed.

"Unk Jesh," Jeremy said.

As Maureen had several errands to run— it was difficult getting things done with Jeremy under one arm— she asked me to take him down to the beach. It was only four blocks away and there was a nice boardwalk. I could take Jeremy down in the stroller and then lock it to a post while he played.

On the stroll down Jeremy was quiet; he jangled the set of keys to the house Maureen had loaned me. The neighbourhood was quiet in the morning, the trees heavy with leaves, the ponderous porches of the houses vacant and still. Jeremy must have been familiar with the beach, for he grew excited and restless as we approached. I chained the stroller, took off my shoes and socks and then Jeremy's, and we started along the boardwalk. He raised his hand for me to hold it. I had to stoop slightly. "Bird," he said, pointing to a seagull standing on the corner stump of a pier. "That's right," I said. "A seagull."

"Seagull," he said.

The wooden boards felt cool and pleasant under my feet, even the stray grains of sand. Jeremy seemed to like it too. He chattered on and pointed to things. Often I didn't understand but answered with interest anyway. His bare feet were beautiful. Sometimes he became confused and called me "Daddy," but usually he just said "Jesh."

"Oh look," he squealed. "Boat. A big boat."

"Where?" I shaded my eyes and looked toward the water. On the horizon was a freighter, but faint.

"See it?" Jeremy asked.

"Yes, I do," I said. "It's very far away. Let's wave to the people on the boat."

I waved my hand. Jeremy followed, very solemnly, as if saying goodbye to a friend.

When we got home Maureen was waiting at the window. She came onto the drive and swept Jeremy up into her arms. She had been crying.

"I missed him," she said.

IN THE AFTERNOON I went out to attend some business of my own. But I came back in time to have dinner with Maureen and Jeremy. In his bed Jeremy wanted me to read him a story. I chose a book of nonsense rhymes that Edward had bought. Jeremy liked the sounds of the words. He fell asleep. When I came down again Maureen and I watched the news. She talked about buying a new coat for him. Then she excused herself and went to her room. I stayed up and read from one of the few books on the shelf.

Each day of the week passed in the same way. I would take Jeremy to the beach or the park while Maureen went shopping or to get her hair cut. In the afternoon I left them alone until dinner time. I felt as if I had been here more than just a few days.

On Friday morning I took Jeremy to the boardwalk. Today he wanted to play on the beach and we walked down to just above the water's edge and sat on the damp sand. Jeremy dug a hole with a stick. He found several stones that glistened when I washed them in the water and made me put them in my pocket to take home. We sang three songs, first "Baa Baa Black Sheep," then "Twinkle Twinkle Little Star" and then his favourite, "Happy Birthday to You." He clapped his hands after each song. Sometimes he smiled or said "Jesh" for no reason.

When we got up our trousers were wet. Jeremy tried to brush the sand off his behind. "Oh oh," I said.

He looked at me. "Oh oh," he said.

The two of us together, "Oh oh."

When we got home Maureen was getting Jeremy's lunch ready. We stood in the hallway with guilty looks on our faces. "What have you two been up to?" she said.

"We're wet!" Jeremy said. And he ran into her arms.

In the evening I read to Jeremy, sitting on the edge of his small bed. When I started to read he shook his head.

"Then what do you want me to read?" I asked.

"Daddy."

"But we don't have any book like that."

"Daddy."

"All right," I said. He lay down with his hand pushed against his lower lip and pretended to close his eyes.

"Let me tell you about how your Daddy and I built a treehouse in the back yard."

"House," Jeremy said.

"That's right, a house high up in a tree. Naturally it was your Daddy's idea..."

After Jeremy fell asleep I kissed him on the forehead and went downstairs. Maureen had the evening paper spread on the coffee table; she was looking for a part-time job. By the telephone lay my airline ticket. I was supposed to phone the airline and reserve a seat for tomorrow.

"I'm tired," I said.

"So am I," Maureen said, yawning. She folded the paper and got up.

"Should I turn out the light?"

"Please do," she said.

At the market we bought pomegranates, the last of the season, and took them back to our room. Inside they were blood-red and wet as tears.

I remember Virginia Woolf: "as if to be caught happy in a world of misery was for an honest man the most despicable of crimes." But today I recognize only the shape of you moving under the sheets, the hat on the knob, a purple glow behind the curtains.

The Other Journal

WHAT A GOOD IDEA this is! I press pen to paper— new pen, and new paper too, a hand-bound journal, the cover leather, the pages a rich cream. S. has an identical one. Well, of course, I gave it to her. It was my idea to write in these journals every morning, to record our impressions on this trip. S. hesitated at first— no, she was positively resistant, almost excessively so. "But I haven't written anything in years," she complained. She thinks I have an advantage, as I'm always writing briefs, memos, reports, contracts. And it's true I've never had trouble with words. But I was afraid that S. would be a little bored, since I have to spend part of each day working.

And there she is— there *you* are— staring down at your open journal with a look that is really pitiful. A look of blankness almost, your mouth slightly open. I know just what you're thinking: "How can I fill these beautiful pages with my petty thoughts?" But that's what they're for, love! Your own journal to write whatever you wish.

As for mine: the coffee is excellent, the croissant melts in my mouth, and the view of the courtyard is pleasant. Bricks, vines, chairs, a fountain (not working). What else? I myself have never been much for description; even now I always skip dull passages in novels. Today is the first meeting with the *syndicat*. I must appear friendly but determined, desirous of success but only on terms much closer to our position. Then when our differences have been narrowed a swift move to lock the whole thing up— what I like to call "the courage to close the deal." But then that's what I'm good at. That's why they've sent me.

A thought: ask the front desk to send up the *International Herald Tribune* in the mornings.

Ah— there! S. writes her first words (I've been keeping half an eye on her). But so gently, as if afraid of tearing the exquisite paper. She makes a face and crosses out a word. No, the whole line! Poor S. You must try again.

The weather is cool and cloudy. We have only five days, the board needs the agreement signed by then or the bank pulls out. But still I should have half the day free to take S. around. She's never seen Paris and it's like a second home to me. I see she has begun writing again. How slowly, like an invalid learning to walk. But a little introspection will do her good.

A question: is it proper to ask for a second cup of coffee? If I want it, why not!

TUESDAY

THIS MORNING S. forgot her journal in the room and had to go back up to fetch it. But she opened it immediately and started to write, without even putting jam on her croissant. As if she had been thinking of what to put down.

Yesterday the Musée D'Orsay. Bronze sculptures, the Impressionists, the big clock overlooking the café. Personally, I find the architecture more interesting than the paintings: train station as relic of industrial power. And I was impressed by how the French invest in their tourist industry. Of course they'd be stupid not to. All those dead artists are a gold mine.

S. has hardly said two words to me this morning. Look at her write! Good girl. Get it all down, those breathless impressions of Monet and Renoir. Can't tell if she's enjoying herself, she looks so serious. Now she pauses to shake her hand loose and begins again. It's wonderful to see her so— so intense.

The *syndicat* people were very polite, very formal; a good thing I brought my black jacket. Had to laugh at their jokes, half of which I didn't understand. S. didn't say very much at lunch, not even to the wives. She showed them some postcards she bought, which they pretended to admire. Poor S., she's always so trusting. I really have to watch over her.

And still she's writing. Now she looks up and smiles absently, as if she doesn't really see me. "Darling," she says. "Are these journals private, or for sharing after?"

"Whatever you like," I say. And then, "No, let's make them private. It's more fun."

"Yes," she says. "It's more fun."

Today we're going to walk in the Bois de Boulogne. According to the papers, the markets are edgy, especially New York and Tokyo. I don't know what else to write, but S. hasn't stopped yet. Now she caps her pen and closes the journal, slipping it into her handbag.

"You don't want to carry that around all day," I say.

"Oh, you never know," she shrugs. "I might want to write something down."

"You see?" I smile. "Weren't they a good idea?"

She looks past me at the dry fountain. "Yes," she says. "You were right as usual."

WEDNESDAY

THIS MORNING the porter forgot to bring up the *Tribune*. When I said something he just tilted his head in that idiotic French way, as if he were humouring a child. Must remember to complain to the manager.

I could hardly drag S. out of the Musée Rodin yesterday, she was so caught up in all that "creative energy." She seemed particularly excited by a few works of Camille Claudel, apparently Rodin's lover. She kept asking why we had never heard of this Camille Claudel. "I don't know," I said. "Lousy publicist?" She didn't appreciate the joke. I spent my time calculating how much all the art owned by the state was worth, but the figure became ridiculous. Why don't they sell some of the lesser stuff to pay off the national debt? No one would even notice.

What *is* she writing? Yesterday evening S. bought a new pen, saying that the one I gave her was already drying up. I took her in to one of those *papeteries*, full of beautiful writing supplies. Wanted to buy her a Waterman fountain pen, but instead she picked an ordinary ball-point and insisted on paying for it herself.

Now this morning she pauses only to say, "It writes just fine."

What *is* she writing about? Cubism? The Latin Quarter? Me? Are there so many thoughts that she can't or won't share with me? This writing has become obsessive. If I thought it would work, I'd suggest we stop. But I know she'd resent it.

Damn it, what are people supposed to write in journals anyway? The weather? That the *syndicat* negotiators are very elegant sons-of-bitches? That everywhere on the street you have to be careful not to step in dog turd?

But I keep writing because she does. I write, I write, I write...

THURSDAY

LAST NIGHT we made love.

There, something intimate to write down. I'm sure S. won't write about it, not when she can't even talk to me about such things. But this journal has no censor. We did it twice, front and back, and afterwards S. fell asleep.

In the night I woke up, needing to piss. S. just turned over. I looked in her bag for her journal, but I didn't find it. Nor in her suitcase either. Is she hiding it from me? Something disturbing about that. It's dishonest and untrusting.

And today something new. S. places one arm on the table, apparently a casual position, but in fact to prevent me from peeking at what she writes. What's truly funny is that I'm not even really interested! It's simple curiosity, that's all, like wanting to know what you're getting for your birthday present.

The way she keeps it up without a pause. She's developed a sort of rhythm, as if her pen is just keeping up with her thoughts. This is unbearable. Silently I plead: tell me what you are writing. Tell me! It's killing me! Why do I feel so vulnerable? Am I such a terrible person to live with? It's true, sometimes I can be selfish, and when I'm in a particularly foul mood I might belittle the way you spend your time, with your part-time job, your classes, your friends. But maybe that's because of all the crap I have to swallow at the office, did you ever think of that? I know I haven't told you how I feel for a long time, not really. I'm living in a kind of fog, I see that now. But I *will* tell you, what you mean to me, at least I'll try.

S., S., what are you writing?

FRIDAY

I'M SORRY, S.

I'm sorry I tore your journal.

But it was the way you took it out of your bag last night, just as we were getting ready to sleep. I was sitting on the edge of the bed, pulling off my socks. I was saying something, I don't remember what now, and turned around to see you open it up and start to write. How stupid it must have looked, us pulling back and forth on the journal like that, until I tore the page.

You were left with it in your hands. And I started weeping, sitting on the bed, with one sock off. I never cried like that in my life. It was strange, I didn't know that crying hurt, physically I mean. You turned off the light and came around to comfort me. Undressed me. And we made love, but so differently from the night before. All night long I slept in your arms.

Perhaps you're writing about it now in your journal. Or maybe you're just describing how the waiter throws crumbs into the dry fountain and the sparrows come down from the vines. I don't know and I don't want to know.

Not that it doesn't matter. It does matter. Today is our last day. I've cancelled lunch with the *syndicat* people. To hell with them. How do I know this change will last, when I hardly even know what it is? As a small sign of faith I put down my pen, for I've had enough of journal writing. But you go on, S., perhaps you'll even continue tomorrow and the day after. Yes, I leave it to you with relief. Write, S. Write down everything.